# Packard's

# Pocketbook

Illustrated by E. P. Henrichs and B.J. Henrichs

Character Ideas by Z. E. Henrichs

Edited by B J. Henrichs

Cover Design by E. P. Henrichs

©2026 E.P. Henrichs


ISBN- 979-8-9916620-2-4

# Characters

Joey Packard – Main character, NOPD Detective, Narrator

Roc – Joey's partner and buddy, brother to Ks

Ks (pronounced K·S) – Joey's partner and more hyperactive buddy, brother to Roc

Radford Weston – Joey's good friend and detective partner, Senior NOPD Detective

Chief Albert A. Anderson – New Orleans Chief of Police

Chief Kurt Allen – New Orleans Chief of Harbor Police

Officer Nathan Richards – Loyal NOPD officer

Officer Jimmy Davis – Friendly gentleman, K-9 handler

Captain Stacy Sharon – Captain of the 6th District

Sean McChain – NOPD Detective

Owen Rohden – NOPD Detective

Officer Garrison – Grizzled, but friendly gentleman, NOPD officer

Tommy Lee – Best friend to Ricky, co-host of the YouTube channel, "The Dudes' Discoveries"

Ricky – Best friend to Tommy Lee, host of the YouTube channel, "The Dudes' Discoveries"

Antonio and Elena López – Millionaire couple from Spain; gained world recognized fame by moving their family and wealth to New Orleans

# The Mail Heist

I took a drink of water and set the glass down on the patio table. I had just finished reading a chapter of Gulliver's Travels. The warm, spring sun shone down brightly in an angular direction, but the cool wind balanced the heat.

Radford's summer home, a 1920's, two-story house which had been refurbished, was a perfect place to spend the weekends. The whole home was whitewashed until it literally shone in the sun. It had blue accents on the shutters, awning, and doors to contrast with the white, and the entrance had large pillars supporting the balcony above.

Mr. Buck, a good friend of ours, had bought the house in rough condition. He fixed up the place and put it up for auction. Radford won the bid, and with the help from Chief Anderson, he bought the house.

I looked around the yard. Radford was trimming the podocarpus, which ran along the long driveway like a snake, and had made his way to the mailbox. Radford enjoyed the landscaping work and was becoming quite skilled with the hedge trimmer.

I leaned back in the patio chair and set the book over my eyes. It was time for a good nap. I slowly began to drift into sleep.

*Clang!*

I jerked out of my slumber and nearly jumped out of my chair. Radford had slammed the hedge trimmer on the table. A look of frustration seethed in his eyes.

"You're done already?" I asked, "Weren't you just out by the mailbox?"

"I was," Radford huffed. He sat down in the other chair next to the table, "I checked the mail after I was done but there was no mail."

I raised an eyebrow, "...And that made you this upset?"

"You don't understand how long I have been waiting," Radford answered, "I ordered a new debit card since my last one was stolen, but it's been a week and it's still not here."

"Ah, Radford," I chuckled, "maybe it's delayed. You know the mail gets held up at times."

"Maybe, but I have been checking daily on the USPS's website, and as of last night, it still doesn't say delivered. I haven't had a mail delay this long in a coon's age. I feel something's happened to it. Anyway, lemme check the papers."

Radford pulled the morning newspaper out of his overalls pocket that he had picked up off the driveway. He removed the plastic bag and set it on the table.

Licking his fingers, he began scanning through the paper.

"Not even the papers have anything on missing mail," he grumbled, "and I checked the city's Facebook pages, and they don't have anything to say either."

"As I said, probably just a delay," I reassured him.

"No, I'm starting to agree with Radford!"

We turned to the voice that came from the next house over. Mr. Jefferson, Radford's neighbor, was hollering over the white picket fence which surrounded Radford's house.

"I haven't had any mail show up for the last few days," Mr. Jefferson complained, "I ordered a few packages for my truck, and they still haven't shown up."

"When did you order them?" Radford asked.

"Last Monday, should've been here by now."

"Goodness gracious," Radford grumbled getting out of his chair. He swiped up his hedge trimmer and hustled to the front door.

"Where are you going?" I asked, turning around in my chair.

"To check the USPS website again," Radford replied, "I'm going to see if there's an update on that card!"

I got up and followed him into the house. Radford wasn't the quickest on his feet, but when he was determined, there was extra pep in his step. Radford set down his hedge trimmer by the door and swiftly made his way to the computer. The computer was on the living room coffee table. It was occupied by the rocks, and from what I could tell, they were playing a game.

"Move rocks!" Radford demanded. He looked at the coffee table, which was covered in headphones and a microphone, "What's all this?"

"But, but..." Ks protested, "we're playing Solitaire. We are in an online Solitaire league chatting with other members."

"That can wait," Radford said, waving them away with his hands, "I need the computer now. Now, shoo!"

"Alright, alright," Roc complained as he and Ks hopped off the table, "Don't boil your beans."

Radford took the laptop and plopped down on the couch. He began typing away vigorously. He pulled up the USPS's website and navigated to package tracking. He typed in his tracking number and waited for a few seconds. I counted the seconds as we waited.

"See! I told you!" Radford snorted.

"What? What is it?" I asked, leaning in to see the screen better.

"It says here that my package has been delivered!" Radford fumed.

I squinted at the monitor, and sure enough it said the mail had been delivered.

"You're right, it does say it's delivered..."

"And the mail isn't here, I checked!" Radford got up, "Follow me youngin."

Radford swiftly stepped out the front door and I hurried along to keep up. We walked down the driveway to the mailbox. Radford stopped right in front of it and opened the lid.

"Look in there and tell me I'm not crazy," he ordered.

I looked in the mailbox. There was no mail. "You're right, there isn't any mail in here..."

"Stick your hand inside and confirm there's none," Radford interrupted.

"But I can clearly see that there isn't..."

"Stick your hand in and feel around for the mail!" Radford repeated.

I shrugged and felt inside the mailbox. Still no mail.

"Nope, nothing," I confirmed.

"See? See?" Radford paced back and forth, "I knew something happened with the mail."

"Well, you are right about it being delayed," I shut the mailbox, "Maybe it's delayed on this street? But it is odd that the website said it was delivered."

"Exactly!" Radford threw up his hands, "It's unacceptable! Come on, we're gonna get to the bottom of it!"

Radford began walking at full speed to his truck. I quickly followed him.

"Where are we heading?" I asked, "It can't be the police station...it's our day off!"

"We're going to ask around the neighborhood," Radford replied, "We're gonna make sure no one else is experiencing mail problems."

I ran to the front door of the house and called in, "Come on, rocks! Radford's on a mission!"

"You two will need your coats," Ks said, running to the coat rack.

"No, we won't be needing them!" Radford hollered from the truck.

I looked at the rocks as we all shrugged. We ran to Radford's red, 1950

Chevy pickup truck and clambered in. Radford cranked the key, and the truck sputtered to life. We backed out of the driveway and rolled down the road. I could feel we were on the edge of another mystery.

*   *   *

1:42 PM

We had been driving around the neighborhood for nearly an hour, getting different stories from folks about their mail. We were at our twentieth house, home to an elderly gentleman who owned a video game store, Mr. Dalton.

"Come to think of it, I'm missing my mail, too," Mr. Dalton rubbed his chin, "It's been a few days since I had any deliveries."

"Do you have anything important missing?" I asked, "Like a credit card or bank statements?

"No... can't think of any...no wait, I actually do have something of some importance being mailed here."

"What is it?" Radford asked.

"My insurance documents," Mr. Dalton responded, "I am switching insurance companies for my store and was needing to go over the paperwork."

"My word," Radford said, "You're at least the twentieth house we've visited that has had important mail delayed, possibly stolen, from them. Something odd is going on here..."

"I wish you gentlemen good luck solving this situation," Mr. Dalton said. He shook Radford's hand. "You will need it!"

We left Mr. Dalton's house and headed back to Radford's truck. I was starting to understand Radford's concern. Something wasn't right. The rocks interrupted my thinking.

"Oooh!" they exclaimed, pointing to the sky, "Would you look at that!"

I looked at the sky and was in awe myself. A full circle rainbow of ice crystals was across a few wispy clouds in the sky

"Oh, glory," I explained, "We were so absorbed in our mystery that I didn't notice that."

"Now's not the time for weather gazing," Radford said with a wave of his hand, "We've got more important things to address."

I noticed Ks about to raise his hand in protest, but he decided against it.

We followed Radford to his truck and clambered in. Radford cranked the key.

"Well," Ks spoke up over the low rumble of the engine, "It seems like someone has been stealing mail."

"And they've been only stealing mail with value," Roc added, "Because who would want someone else's magazine subscriptions?"

"Definitely," I agreed, "We'll have to take all this into consideration when we get back to work Monday."

"Nuh uh," Radford shook his head, "We're solving this case now."

"What!?" The rocks exclaimed, "On our weekend off?"

I was quite surprised as well. "You really think we will have time to solve this debacle, Radford?"

"Ohhh sure," Radford said, "we've got plenty of time. The mail doesn't come until five in the evening. We've got the rest of today and tomorrow if need be."

I looked at the rocks and shrugged. I turned to Radford, "Okay, I guess what we're gonna have to do is a stakeout on some of the mailboxes around here."

Radford nodded. "We won't be able to cover the whole town, obviously, so we'll just stake out the neighborhood of Uptown we investigated. There's four of us, so each one of us can watch a mailbox."

"Alrighty, " said Ks, "Sounds good, let's go!"

"Wait," Radford stopped him, "I got plans to make our jobs even more efficient. We need to first find homes which are expecting valuable mail to come in. If our hunch is true, the thieves will only take that mail, like debit cards, money, insurance papers, bank statements, all that jazz..."

"Makes sense," I agreed, "But maybe we should have one of us watch a house that won't get valuable mail, to be one hundred percent certain that our thieves are going after the valuable mail."

"That's a good idea actually, I can watch my summer house tomorrow since I ain't getting any important mail. Let's first find the homes expecting important mail and then we'll head back to the house. We can devise our plans there."

*   *   *

4:10 PM

We were back at Radford's summer house a few hours later. We had already found a few houses that were going to receive valuable mail, now we were mapping out the neighborhood streets where we would station ourselves. Radford would post his stakeout in front of his summer house on St. Charles Avenue. Ks would be waiting on Chestnut Street; I would be positioned at a block in Constance Street with Roc on Coliseum Street. The streets were in close proximity to each other, so if anyone was going around and stealing mail, one of us would see them.

"That seals the deal," Radford stretched and closed his laptop lid.

"We're all set, lads. Tomorrow the mail comes in around noon, so that gives us plenty of time to get set up."

Radford opened the coffee table drawer and pulled out two walkie-talkies and a flip phone. He handed a talkie to Ks, and the other talkie, along with the flip phone, to Roc.

"Joey and I will communicate through our phones," he said, "Roc, you and Ks communicate through the talkies, and whatever information Ks gives you, you give that information to Joey. He will then give it to me."

"A stroll in the garden," Roc grinned, "Sounds like a plan."

"And also, take these," Radford pulled out two cameras, "You two need to take pictures for proof. If you see them, that is. Joey and I can already take pictures with our phones."

"I gotta hand it you, Radford," I said, "This is a good little plan you got going on."

"Thanks, sonny," Radford replied, "We're gonna need a good plan to catch these crooks in the act."

"If there are any crooks in the first place," Ks added.

"Trust me, Ks," Radford said, getting up from the couch, "This is definitely the work of mail thieves. All evidence points towards it, we now just need proof."

"Well, let's go pick out our spots in the streets," I said, "We're gonna need to sleep early tonight."

*　　*　　*

5:14 PM

I sat in my car at a block in Constance Street, positioned in a street across from my target house. I waited patiently watching the house's mailbox. I looked at the time; half an hour had passed since we all got into our stakeout positions. I knew we'd have to wait a bit with this one, since not many people would steal mail immediately after the postal service just dropped it off. I drummed my fingers on the steering wheel, keeping a watchful eye on the mailbox.

The phone ringing in my hand brought me out of my staring. It was Roc, so. I quickly answered.

"Yo Roc, what do you got?"

"Ks just called me. He said he saw a man and a woman in a white van stop at the house he's watching. They rummaged through the mailbox but didn't take anything. They drove to the next house and did the same. Ks said they kept checking mailboxes until they were out of his sight."

"That might prove Radford's suspicions about thieves taking mail of value," I said.

"Yeah, it makes sense they are taking the mail during Saturday afternoon. A lot of people are out at restaurants for dinner."

"Right. Keep an eye out, 'cause our streets are close to Ks' street. They should be coming down our roads soon."

"Alrighty, I'll call back immediately if I see them."

Roc hung up. I quickly called Radford and told him all the information. Radford let out a loud hooray on the other side of the line. I winced as it pierced my ear. Radford isn't usually a loud man, but he can be when he wants to!

"I told you! I knew something was happening!" He said with triumphant vigor, "we got them varmints now!"

The phone suddenly buzzed against my ear. I checked the phone and saw Roc was trying to call again.

"Gotta go, Radford," I explained, "Roc is calling me back."

I hung up on Radford and answered Roc's call.

"I see them!" Roc exclaimed, "A white Chevy van is driving down my street! The occupants are looking through the mailboxes. They rummaged through the mailbox from the house I am watching, and took some items, but left the rest behind!"

"Same white van?" I asked.

"Same one just as Ks described; color, the couple, everything."

"Okay, this is good! We got some good evidence on our hands. Remember to take pictures!"

"Oh right, I nearly forgot! Be alert, they'll be heading down your road soon."

Roc hung up and I pulled up the camera app on my phone. I was now watching the road like a hawk, knowing they could pop up any minute now. Several cars drove by my location: a black Dodge Charger, a Chevy Volt, a Nissan truck, a white Chevy van. I sat up instantly. A white van! Holding up my phone, I was ready to snap a few pictures of the van.

The van pulled up to the front of the house and parked. It was the newer model and in good condition. It sat there for several minutes, but no one got out. I could see a man and a woman looking in their review mirrors. Were they making sure the coast was clear? The duo finally got out and began to rummage through the mailbox. The man looked to be in his early forties and had reddish brown hair. Surprisingly, he looked like he was dressed in a suit and tie. The woman looked in her mid-thirties, and from what I could see, she also looked well dressed. After some searching, they pulled out a small package and left the other mail behind. I was so itching to arrest them there on the spot, but we were off the clock, and we also couldn't blow our cover. I snapped multiple photos of the couple and the van. They hurried back inside the van and drove to the next mailbox. They repeated this procedure to all the mailboxes down the street until they were out of sight.

I quickly dialed up Radford and told him everything I saw.

"Be alert," I cautioned, "They might be headed down your street any minute now."

"Oh, don't you worry," Radford fumed, "I got my eyes peeled!"

"Remember, don't let you anger blow your cover!"

I could only wait in silence now, hoping Radford would keep his emotions in control, or he would blow the investigation. We would have enough evidence to arrest the couple if Radford blew his cover, but it would just be better if everything went according to our plan. Suddenly, Radford called me back.

"I've had enough!" he bellowed, "They are taking all of my neighbor's mail! I'm *gonna put them under a citizen's arrest!"*

"Radford, wait-!" I began, but it was too late, he already cut me off.

I quickly put the car into drive and sped towards St. Charles Street. I hoped Radford knew what he was doing! I had to remind myself he was a very experienced senior detective. I drove around the block and onto St. Charles Street. I called the rocks while on my way and told them what Radford was doing. I soon arrived at Radford's house and saw the white van parked by the mailbox. I saw the man and woman kneeling on the sidewalk, next to the van, with their hands on their heads. Radford had them both at gunpoint with his derringer while talking on the phone. I switched the gear into park and grabbed my cuffs and ran over to the van. Radford had finished got off his phone and gave me a triumphant grin.

"Haha!" he boomed, "We got 'em! I told ya someone was behind all of this!"

"Geesh, Radford!" I cuffed the two suspects, "You could've waited for us before you detained these two."

"Time, my friend," Radford said, holstering his gun. "It's all about time! I couldn't let these mail thieves escape!"

I helped the man and woman up and told them to lean against the van. Roc and Ks came running down the street and joined us. We couldn't question the two since we were off duty, so we waited for the officers Radford had called earlier. They were distraught, constantly begging to be released. It was a usual criminal response, any person caught in their position would do the same.

After a few minutes, my coworkers Officers Nathan Richards, David Dawson, and Megan Monroe showed up. We turned the two over to the officers so they could be questioned. Richards read them their Miranda rights and began questioning.

"What's your and your wife's name, sir?"

"She's not my wife yet, sir" the man replied, "She's, my girlfriend. I'm Regan and this is Reilly."

"What are you two doing out here stealing mail? That's a foolish thing to do, y'know. You might get someone really angry, and you could get yourselves hurt."

"We didn't want to..." Reilly blurted out, "We were forced to by some...them."

"Forced to steal mail?" Officer Dawson spoke up, "By who?"

Regan and Reilly fell silent, they both stared at the ground. I looked at Radford and the rocks in confusion.

"You're not gonna tell us who?" Richards asked again, but the two didn't talk anymore.

"We can't..." Regan muttered, "They'll kill us..."

"Some story," Dawson scoffed.

"I agree," said Richards, "I assume you two are done talking. Let's go."

The officers put the two in the back of their squad cars. A few other officers pulled up and began shuffling through the mail in the van. That was it; for the most part, it was all over. All that was left to do was appear in court and give our statements and findings. I turned to Radford and the rocks.

"Well, that wraps up that little episode."

"Yep," agreed Ks, "But what kind of story was that they tried to spin? No one would be that desperate for mail that they would force folks to steal it."

"And also threaten to kill them if they told anyone." Roc added.

"That's just how it is," Radford said, "Being in this line of work for thirty years, I hear all kinds of stories, from pretty believable to plain, outright dumb. It's sad how some people will cause panic and ruin the lives of others just for their own selfish shenanigans. Just despicable. Now excuse me, I'm gonna find my debit card."

Radford walked to the van with the officers and began rifling through the mountain of mail. I looked at the rocks and they looked back at me. Radford said it best, all we could do was nod in agreement.

-Joey Packard

# Dawn of the Night Peddler

It happened all so suddenly one Wednesday night in July, around the eighth hour of the evening. It was a warm, muggy night, and Radford and I were heading home from an evening play we had attended. The play was a spectacular version of Our Town, one of Radford's favorite plays. Radford was fond of plays. Of course, he enjoyed the theatrics and huge blockbusters, but plays were his kind of jazz. Ks and Roc followed behind us, bringing up the rear. We made our way through downtown New Orleans, along the sidewalk, passing many shops displaying goods in their storefront windows.

"So, how did you like that version of Our Town?" I asked.

"It was pretty decent," Radford answered, rubbing his chin, "Though, there were a few elements I liked about the other version we saw last week better than this one. This one was still pretty solid."

I chuckled; Radford was very peculiar about his plays. He had to have all the details follow the original story to the period. "What did you think was better in last week's version?" I asked again.

"Well, the moment Emily goes to the Afterlife," Radford began, "At the moment she was headed there..."

Suddenly, a blood chilling scream broke through the night, abruptly ending our conversation. Our hair stood up on our backs; we all froze in our tracks.

"Great Scott!" Radford shivered, "What was that?"

"That sounded like a woman's scream," I replied. "It can't be more than a few blocks away. Hurry!"

We quickened our pace and trotted down the sidewalk. After turning a few corners, we saw group of people huddled around a woman. The woman was lying on the ground, and for a moment we feared the worst. As we drew nearer, to our relief, we saw that murder wasn't the case. The woman was still breathing, although unconscious. A few people were fanning her with newspapers and bags, trying to revive her. A few saw us walking up and moved aside for us.

"We heard her scream, detectives," a man explained, "we rushed to her aid as we saw her faint."

"Ah, she's coming 'round," a lady in the crowd said with a sigh.

The woman slowly opened her eyes while Radford knelt beside her. She sat up and looked around while the look of panic came back to her face.

"Ma'am, whatever is the matter?"
Radford asked.

"I saw a ghost!" the woman exclaimed
in panicked tones, "It was a figure dressed
in a black cloak, and it was carrying a large
sack on its back. I was on my way home and
it passed right in front of me. Naturally I
screamed and the next thing I knew, I
blacked out! I saw a ghost tonight, I'm
sure of it!"

"Which way did the figure go?" I asked.

The woman pointed to an alley. We all
looked in that direction. It was a dark
alley, barely lit, for the streetlights didn't
penetrate the murky darkness. It was a
one-way alley, meaning it eventually came
to an end due to the back of a shop's wall.
I looked around the crowd; no one dared
venture into the alley.

"I'll take a look," Roc said, holding up his hand, "There must be a rational explanation for all o' this."

Roc walked into the alley with caution and looked around. The alley was about 40 feet long and only 20 feet wide. I assumed a garbage truck could scarcely fit in it. A few trash cans were stationed outside the two shops' back doors, one on the left and one on the right. A dumpster was against the rear facing the wall of the third shop, ready for a trash truck to drive in and empty it. Paper and cardboard boxes lay scattered about.

"Not saying I believe in ghosts," Ks spoke up, "but this might be the one situation to convince..."

"All's good," Roc shouted from the shadows, "There's nothing here!"

"Is there any way it could've escaped," I asked, "Any holes in the wall?"

"Nope, none," Roc answered as he looked around, "The walls are sound."

Radford looked back at the woman. "Are you certain you saw a hooded figure?"

"Yes!" she exclaimed, "I know what I saw!"

"It could've been someone taking out the trash," I suggested, "They could've gone in through the back doors to the shops."

"But Mr. Packard," the woman shivered, "why would someone take out the trash in a black cloak?"

"No one has gone through the doors either," said Roc, jiggling one of the door handles while standing on a trash can. "The doors are still locked. Although someone could have locked the doors..."

However, Roc was leaning too far on the edge trash can, it slipped out from under him, and he fell to the floor with a loud crash. We jumped at the clamor, but eventually we all began to chuckle.

"Ha ha!" Ks laughed, "You were...ha ha...too heavy! You didn't count...ha ha...your own weight!"

"Stop laughing like a buffoon in front of everyone," Roc retorted, "We are investigating serious matters here!"

I decided it was time to reassure the crowd, "It's time we call it a night now, folks. Everything is fine. Whatever ran by here is not here anymore. You all can go about your business. Have a goodnight."

The crowd murmured amongst themselves, but after a brief second, they all began to depart their own ways. I turned to Radford.

"Welp, time we split ways and head home," I said, "We'll see you tomorrow."

"Ah, sure," Radford began, "but first, let's go get a warm tea at the ol' restaurant. I'm still shaken by tonight's experience."

"Alright, old friend," I chuckled, slapping him on the back, "Lead the way!"

With that, we continued our walk down the sidewalk to Brennan's Restaurant.


*   *   *


Friday, 7:40 PM

I set a stack of police paperwork on our large chestnut desk. The desk was an antique, a 1960 Leonardo double pedestal to be exact. It gave a very complete feel to the study, sitting near the large glass window. The window overlooked Canal Street, and the bells of the old retro trolleys could be heard passing by, along with the sound of roaring car engines and beeping horns. Roc came in, followed by Ks, holding a few files of even more paperwork. He walked to the file cabinet and placed the files in the correct slot.

"That's another day of work done," Roc said, "You got all your papers sorted out?"

"I do in fact," I replied, "They're sorted, ready to be handed over to the station tomorrow."

I got off my desk chair and stretched. I must have been sitting for two hours at least getting all the paperwork done. I looked at my watch; it was fifteen 'til eight.

"I'm gonna head to the shop to get that bird seed before it gets too late," I said, "Shouldn't be gone more than ten minutes."

"Alrighty," said Ks, "we'll hold the fort.

I pulled on my trench coat and descended the stairs to the lobby. Miss Jane and Mrs. Mary, the women behind the desk, saw me coming down.

"Where you off to at this hour?" asked Miss Jane.

"Don't tell me you're off on another adventure at this time of night," sighed Mrs. Mary.

"No, of course not, ladies," I reassured them, "I'm off to buy some bird seed for Pauley."

"Whew!" they exclaimed together, "That's a relief."

I chuckled and stepped out of the apartment complex into the night street. It was a beautiful night, although rather hot. The rising moon shone brightly, the only thing in the sky, for the city lights blinded out the stars. I breathed in the city air and headed down the few blocks to the little convenient shop. The town's folk were in a jovial mood tonight, and I generously said hello to each one that passed by. I made it there after only a few minutes' walk.

After about five minutes, I had found the seed we needed and had already purchased it. I had just made my way out the door when I heard terrible screams. The people on the sidewalk froze in their tracks, trying to locate where the screams came from. The screams were that of a man and a woman and sounded as if they were only a few blocks away. I ran in the direction of the screams and found a group of people standing around a man and a woman. My recollections of the other night started to come back to me. The man and woman were shaking with fear, fumbling with their items. The man turned and saw me coming.

"Mr. Packard," he exclaimed, " we both saw a ghost, no doubt about that!"

"A ghost carrying a black sack on its back to be precise!" the woman added.

"Which way did it go?" I asked, having a strong feeling of Deja vu.

"Across the street, into that alley," the man answered, pointing a shaking finger to the alley.

The crowd and I looked across the road. A few people in the crowd shuddered, and I immediately knew why. It was the same alley from the incident a couple nights ago, and a few in the crowd experienced that previous event, as did I.

"Another spirit has come to haunt New Orleans!" a woman in the crowd shouted, arousing a panicked commotion in the crowd.

I began to become intrigued by these incidents. Two sightings within a day of each other, each having similar circumstances. A black cloaked figure carrying a sack on his back, disappearing into the same, small alley. How did it disappear in a small alley with limited places to hide? Why did it only come out at night, preferably at the eighth hour of the evening? Were these two sightings connected or coincidence? I decided it was time to investigate.

*   *   *

Monday, 2:00 PM

My hunch to start investigating the "ghost" sightings was a good one. Over the weekend, a few more reports came in describing a similar figure appear, this time around different parts of Canal

Street. The strange phenomenon eventually made its way into the headlines of the Times-Picayune, the New Orleans paper, and even the local news. The strange figure eventually got a name by the frightened locals, they called it the Night Peddler. I thought the name was very fitting. Chief Anderson had ordered all members of the New Orleans PD in the 8th district to keep an eye out for the Peddler. It wasn't an urgent command, just a small precaution to put the citizens at ease.

Today the two youngins, Ricky and Tommy Lee, were visiting my apartment. They had their fair share of meeting the Peddler.

"I'm telling ya, dude," Ricky explained to me in an anxious tone, "the ghost is real! There is a Night Peddler, and we saw him!"

"He floated along and disappeared into an alley," exclaimed Tommy Lee, "He's out there causing a panic!"

"Don't worry," I reassured them as I led them out the door, "The police is on the lookout. We will find out about the Peddler soon enough. You two go do some skateboarding and have fun."

The two lads still seemed very doubtful, but they took my advice and left. I walked over to the sofa and sat down beside Radford, who was reading the papers. The rocks were tending to Pauley.

"It's strange that there's been more and more sightings of the Peddler over the weekend," Radford said as he flipped through the papers, "It looks like the Peddler is showing his face more often."

"That could be possible," I replied, picking up a paper, "but people are actually looking for the Peddler now since it's local news, so the sightings are definitely going to be more numerous. Our friend the Peddler could have been here all the time."

"True, true," Radford agreed, closing his paper, "It's still incredible all the same."

Radford got up from the sofa and stretched. "I kind of want to see this Peddler fellow myself to be honest," he said while wiping his glasses, "Seems like an ominous fellow."

"We aren't going to have to wait long," I said standing, "because the rocks and I are going see him tonight!"

Ks and Roc turned to us and exclaimed, "We are?" They had the most puzzled look on their faces.

"Correct," I answered and held up a finger, "It's time we get some clarity in this matter."

"How will we know where to look?" Roc asked.

"Well," I began, "a few of the witnesses saw the Peddler head into that alley, remember? It would be a good idea to stakeout that place tonight. Also, I noticed that three of the sightings happened around the eighth hour."

"Okay, the alley at eight o'clock," Ks agreed. He shivered, "I sure do hope the Peddler isn't a spirit that'll haunt us because we are spying on it..."

* * *

7:55 PM

It was a little cooler that night from the rain earlier that day, and a light breeze blew. I was grateful for this, I did not want to sit on a stakeout on a hot, muggy night. Our watch post was a planting strip in the sidewalk across the street from the alley in question. A few mosquitoes buzzed around my ear, and I swatted at them excessively. Ks was swatting at them as well.

"Stop making so much noise you two," Roc grumbled, "You'll blow our cover."

"This is one time where you should be grateful," I said, smacking another mosquito, "You two don't have to worry about them sucking your blood."

"That doesn't matter to me," Ks added, "The buzzing noise alone is driving me crazy...!"

Ks suddenly stopped talking and pointed to the street. Roc and I swiftly looked in the direction of his finger. Like a phantom gliding under the moonlight, there it was, dressed in a black cloak carrying a black sack, the Night Peddler. The rocks and I were petrified with shock.

"No wonder the town's folk were freaking out," whispered Ks, "It's a freaking ghost!"

"And it's heading to the same alley," Roc added.

We watched as the Peddler crossed the road and disappeared into the alley. I motioned to the rocks to leave the median. We ran across the street and stopped in front of the alley. The Peddler was gone; all that was left were a few cardboard boxes, the dumpster, and empty trashcans.

"The townsfolk were right..." Roc said in disbelief.

"The Peddler is a ghost!" Ks exclaimed.

I had my doubts though. I walked into the alley and looked for anything out of the ordinary. There wasn't though; they were the same old items...trashcan, boxes, dumpster. I looked again at the dumpster. Something about it caught my interest. I moved to the side of the dumpster and examined the side. Nothing was unusual looking, just flaked paint. I took out my SD and scanned the dumpster. No, there were no fingerprints. The Peddler was either a ghost...or he used gloves.

"Rocks," I said as I clambered behind the dumpster, "let's move this. I believe there's something underneath it that will give us an answer."

Roc and Ks came to my aid and took up pushing positions. On the count of three, and with a big grunt, we heaved the dumpster out of its position. Aha, there was my answer!

"There's a trapdoor here!" exclaimed Ks.

"Right, just as I assumed," I said, "Our friend the Peddler didn't vanish; he just used this trap door."

"How did he disappear through it so quickly?" asked Roc, "It took us a few pushes to get it out of the way."

"Ah!" I said as I peered into the dumpster, "There's a piece of sheet metal covering a hole cut into the bottom of this dumpster."

"So that explains it," Roc said, putting the pieces together, "The Peddler just hopped into the dumpster and went through the trap door. He didn't disappear at all."

"Right," Ks agreed, "but that still doesn't explain why the Peddler looks like a ghost, or why he only comes out at night."

I grinned, "Time we gather those answers ourselves."

I grabbed the latch to the trapdoor and pulled open the metal door. A ladder was at the entrance, descending into the black void of the underground cellar.

"Ugh..." shivered Ks, "It's dark as a dungeon down there, the moon isn't shining bright enough to penetrate that murky gloom."

"Yep, too dark to see anything," I added and took out our SD. I turned on its light and aimed it down the ladder, "This should give us adequate light."

We slowly descended the stairs guided by the SD's light. The stairs only reached about eight feet below the surface of the ground. The cellar was small, only about nine feet wide and filled with crates. We were confused; why were there crates down here? I suspected the obvious; these crates were full of narcotics. Suddenly, something long and thin dragged over my shoulder.

"Spigots!" I jumped while vigorously swiping it off my shoulder, "What was that?"

"It's just a string to a light bulb," Roc said, pointing upwards.

I looked up and saw the bulb. I was relieved. I pulled on the string and the dim light bulb lit up the cellar. We looked around and studied the crates. We all now assumed that the crates contained drugs.

"Well, guess this Peddler is peddling drugs," Ks spoke up, "But where is he? He must have vanished again."

"Either he's a ghost..." I said, "...or he has another room here."

I looked around the cellar searching for a door or small passageway. To my satisfaction, there was one hidden between two crates. I cautiously opened the door and peered in. Ks and Roc looked through the door as well. The room was small, lit with only a single bulb. A small table was at the end of it and seated on a stool in front of the table was the Peddler. He was hunched over the table, doing some sort of paperwork. He was wearing a black-hooded tunic and leather medieval boots. I was amused, this guy looked like he was completely in the wrong time period. Beside him on the ground was the famous sack, which garnered him his namesake. I held a finger to my lips, and we slowly crept in. I raised my hands above the Peddler and grabbed his shoulders. He jolted out of his seat and fell over the desk to the ground, holding his chest. I could now see that he wore a black mask that covered the greater part of his face.

"Oh me, oh my!" he said in a very southern, high-pitched voice, "Don't do that, detective! Ya nearly struck me to death with panic!

"That's only half the panic you've been causing the city," I retorted, "what are you doing running around at night dressed like a ghost?"

"I ain't doin' any crime," he whimpered, "I'm dressed like this to conceal my identity while I sell my stuff."

"Selling drugs you mean," I said.

"Oh no, no, no!" He held up his hands, "I'm a man of mystery, not a man of crime. I'm selling mints to people."

I wrinkled my eyebrow in confusion, "Mints?"

"He's right," said Roc. He and Ks were digging through the sack, "It's only mints, I mean... at least they look like Lifesavers mints."

"Yes," the Peddler said, he was speaking very quickly, "I have a market for these mints. I run a Facebook group, and people all over the city come for my mints."

"Why do they come to you for mints," I asked in bewilderment, "can't they just buy them from the store in bulk?"

"It is because my mints are some the best aroun' here," the Peddler answered, "I've found a way to mix in powder made from the finest of healthy, bountiful herbs. They are nature's medicine, and I have it here, in my mints."

I was genuinely confused, impressed, and a little skeptical all at once. "But why the hiding in a black cloak, and why hide down here in this bunker?" I asked.

"That is obvious, Mr. Packard," he replied, "I need to hide the contents in this here bunker so no one can steal my product. And I run this whole peddler thing for originality, for the fun of it. Ain't no one in this town who's gonna forget the Night Peddler anytime soon."

I pondered what was told to me for a good moment, and then I picked up one of the mints out of the sack. Each mint was white and round with a hole in the center, just like a Lifesaver. They were individually wrapped as well.

"Well, Mr. Peddler, we're gonna have to take a few of these in for inspection," I chuckled, "It's the standard protocol; I don't know if you're a man of genuine business or a liar. And please, try not to be so ominous, you're scaring the town's folk shirtless."

"Oh yes, of course, Mr. Detective," he said clasping his hands together, bowing slightly, "By all means, do your duties. You'll find nothing but the highest quality mint and herbs. I will try to be less of a frightening presence from now on."

I nodded and grabbed a few mints from the sack. The Peddler waved at us as the rocks and I left through the door.

                    *    *    *



To the Peddler's merit, the results came out just as he said they would. The mints were made of a mixture of Echinacea and Biden herbs with Swiss mint leaves. No illegal substances were found in the mints, so we didn't have anything to charge against him. Chief Anderson had wanted to see the bunker for himself, but when I took him there last night, everything was gone. The crates full of mints, the desk and stool, the Peddler himself, vanished into thin air. It was evident that he had moved his stash to another spot, hidden away from the eyes of the world once again.

"There's been no sightings of the Peddler recently," Radford said as he shut off the TV. We had just finished watching the local news while Ks and Roc played Solitaire on the coffee table. Radford began wiping his glasses, "Things seem to have calmed down now."

"It seems he took my advice quite well," I grinned, "He's not being such a spook on the streets anymore."

"That was some of the strangest nonsense that's happened recently," said Ks as Roc placed another card down.

"That was one of the strangest incidents I've seen in my years of detective work," Radford added.

I had to agree with them both, these recent events were indeed bizarre. And now that the Peddler had vanished once again, that whole feeling of mystery was back. I wish at the time we had him remove his mask, but we didn't. That pushes the mystery surrounding this figure even further. I wondered if we would ever see him wandering the streets again. As I write this, I am still wondering that even now.

-Joey Packard

# The Laughing Witches

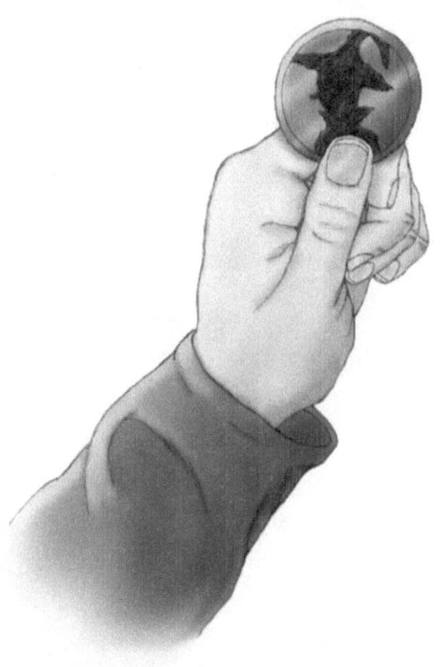

Muggy, humid, and hot. That was the New Orleans weather in August. The moisture clung to your skin, and not even the warm summer breeze could drive it away. Sweat dripped down my brow and stung my eyes. I wiped it away with my sleeve. No one would think that wearing a trench coat in summer would be a practical idea, but it did a good deal of keeping the sun from baking your skin.

Radford stood next to me, fanning himself with his hat. We had only been observing the crime scene for a quarter of an hour, but we were already roasting away. The crime itself was a whole other situation all together. Before us was a mess of a wreck, involving two cars, twisted into heaps of disfigured metal. NOPD squad cars directed traffic away from the wreck site. It was a hit and run; a suspicious hit and run.

The first car belonged to a member of the city council, Mr. Reginald Worth. His car appeared to have been T-boned as he crossed an intersection. Our victim was carried to the ambulance in a stretcher. He had obtained major injuries, but fortunately, he was alive.

Our second car belonged to who we believed was at fault in the accident. By observing the damage from both cars, and the info from a few helpful bystanders, we concluded that the suspect had deliberately wrecked the victim's car in the intersection. But the most baffling thing was that none of the witnesses saw the suspect leave the scene, if there was even a suspect at all. By the time they got to the second car, the suspect was gone. And an even more creepy detail is that several of the witnesses said they heard the most hideous laugh, coming from the swamp brush, as soon as the wreck subsided. It sounded like a woman laughing, almost like a witch.

Despite the efforts of several officers who made a full sweep of the swamp, no one was found. All that was left was a totaled vehicle. Radford and I were now investigating that totaled vehicle. The airbag and seat were bloodstained, and a small trail of blood lead from the vehicle into the brushy swamp. But all hope wasn't lost, for we knew we could take DNA samples from the blood.

"It sure is an ugly wreck," Radford said, breaking a few moments of silence. We were collecting blood samples.

I nodded, "And it being a deliberate wreck makes it a whole lot uglier."

As we looked, I noticed a small shirt pin in the driver's seat. It had the silhouette of a witch's head on it. Pretty odd, but not important. I turned towards the swamp reeds and called out, "Rocks! You both found anything?"

"Nada!" Ks called back. He and Roc were looking through the swamp brush. "The blood trail and footprints go into the swamp and don't leave it. Even the K9 can't track the scent."

"He's right," agreed Officer Davis, who was nearby with the K9. The K9, Butch, frantically tried to pick up a scent, but was having no luck. "Our suspect either used something to cover their scent, or the swamp made old Butch here lose the scent."

"Hmmm..." I rubbed my chin as my mind raced with questions. How did the suspect disappear?

"We'll know who they are soon enough," Radford piped in as he placed the blood sample in a little plastic bag, "we should get back a DNA result in the next twenty-four hours."

He handed the bag to Officer Donald, "Take this back to the station and have it analyzed."

"A'ight," said Donald, taking the bag. He hopped into his patrol car and sped away to the station.

Radford walked up to me as we finished examining the scene. "This boggles my mind; how can we not find our suspect?"

"I'm boggled right along with you, friend," I replied, as we looked around at the scene.

"Well, it's high time we had this mess cleaned up, and allow the traffic to flow through again," Radford said, "we have our photos of the scene and blood samples, all we gotta do now is get the results and piece it together."

*　　*　　*

4:00 PM

I set down a few folders on the desk. Running a hand through my hair, I opened a folder and took a deep breath. It was time to work on the collision case. I sat down and was ready to get my feet wet when Radford and the rocks burst in through the door.

"Joey," Radford said with a breath, "There's been a shooting!"

I immediately jumped out of my chair, "A shooting? Where?"

"In Bourbon Street," Radford answered, "Officers from District 8 are already on the scene. Anderson needs us out there!"

"Right!" I turned to the rocks and handed Ks the folders, "You two take these files to detectives Sharry and Owen and help them figure out this case."

"Aye aye!" Ks said, and he and Roc ran out of the room.

I grabbed my coat and ran out of the room, with Radford leading the way. We exited the station and clambered into Radford's car. Radford revved the engine, and we took off towards Bourbon Street. A few minutes' drive later, we pulled into Bourbon Street. Several of our units and an ambulance were lined up outside a three-story apartment complex, with their lights ablaze. Radford parked the car behind one of our units and we scrambled out of the car. I opened the trunk and pulled out our equipment case. We hurried to the scene where EMS were gathered around the victim. He was put on a stretcher and immediately wheeled to the ambulance, which sped away from the scene and raced to the hospital.

"Poor soul," Radford off took his hat, "A horrible thing, a shooting is."

"I know," I agreed. After a moment of silence, I spoke up, "Let's get to the bottom of this."

We followed Officer Travis into the apartment building and up to the second floor; the scene of the crime. It was a disturbing one. The apartment had one office room, where the crime had taken place. The contents of a desk were strewn all over the floor: paper, folders, and pens. A laptop was on the ground, its monitor cracked. A handgun was next to the laptop, and Officer Smith, who was in the room, confirmed a few rounds had been shot. Behind the desk and chair was a window, which gave a good view of Bourbon Street. The window had two bullet holes in it, either from a .22 round or 9mm. I asked Travis for the details.

"What it looks like from our initial observation," Travis replied, "the suspect somehow broke into the apartment and used the .22 on the floor to shoot councilman Roderick Federman twice while he was sitting at his desk. Luckily for Federman, the bullets went clean though his shoulder and through the window, so he should be able to make a quick recovery."

I thought hard, and I could see Radford was doing the same. He seemed to know the crime happened differently. Radford walked to the window and studied the holes, lowering and raising his glasses. He made a slight nod to himself and looked around the room again. He hustled over to a bookshelf in line with the window. He scanned each self of the bookshelf and made a slight sound of approval. He turned back to us, with a big grin on his face. I had a pretty good idea from that grin that he had found a solution to this case.

"You all did a pretty good investigation of the scene," Radford said, "but that's not quite what happened."

The officers had a look of surprise on their faces. "Oh, really?" Travis asked.

Radford nodded. "I believe that handgun is actually Federman's. He was shot through the shoulder from behind as he was completing his business. He reached for the gun in his drawer and drew it but fell over the desk."

"Shot through the shoulder from the back?" Travis asked, "but we can clearly see the bullets went through the window, proving they went through the front of him."

"Exactly," said Radford, "the bullets did fly through the window, but he wasn't shot through the front."

I finally caught on to Radford's assumptions. "I think Radford may be right," I said, "Let's see if we can prove it."

I walked across the room to the bookshelf adjacent to the wall. The shelf was positioned in front of the desk across the room. After I thoroughly scoured the shelf up and down, I found what Radford was looking for. Lodged halfway into the spine of a large book were two 9mm bullets. I pulled out the book and presented it to the three.

"As Radford suspected," I began, "the bullets were from a 9mm and were fired through the window."

"You mean, from the outside?" Smith asked.

Radford nodded "From the outside. The bullets were shot through the window, through Federman, and lodged themselves in the books on the shelf."

"And by the trajectory of the bullets, they seem to come from..." I looked through the window and snapped my fingers, "...the roof."

Radford and the officers came to the window as well. Bourbon Street is a narrow street; the apartments aren't that far apart from each other. It wouldn't be impossible for someone in the apartments across the streets to shoot someone. It could easily be done without a rifle either.

"I'm going across to the apartments," I said, hurrying out the door, "Someone definitely shot Federman from one of those apartments!"

I burst out of the building and into the street. I ran across the road and stopped at one of the apartments. Looking back to the apartment with the crime scene, I confirmed this was the apartment I needed to investigate. I pulled on the lobby door, but it was locked. I rapped on the door with my knuckles.

"Who is it!?" Someone shouted from the inside. I could see it was a young woman through the glass.

"New Orleans PD, open up," I responded.

As the door slowly opened the young woman's face peeked through the door.

"Oh, good, the police is here. What do you need, detective?" she asked.

"Good day, ma'am," I replied, "I need to check the roof of this apartment. There's been a shooting in the apartments across the street from this apartment."

"The shooting, right!" she nearly shouted, "I heard the shots. My neighbors and I are the ones who called you. It sounded like it came from our roof. We didn't come out because we weren't sure it was safe."

"Well, it's safe to come out now, the shooting's over. I need to investigate the roof. If what you said is true, we should find evidence that will link it up with our findings at the crime scene."

"Sure, I'll get the owner and he can take you up there."

The woman retreated into the lobby. By now other residents were beginning to creep outside and survey the area. I decided to ask the group some questions on the matter.

"Has anyone else heard the shots or seen the shooter?" I asked.

"Yes sir," a man spoke up, "I heard the shots, sounded like they came from the roof above. I know this might sound strange, but I also heard the faint sound of a woman laughing."

I raised an eyebrow, "Did you say a woman laughing?"

"I heard it too!" another man spoke up, "it sounded just like a witch's cackle!"

"Spigots," I muttered. Another witchy cackle? It seemed like an awfully specific coincidence.

At that moment, the young woman came back to the door with the owner. I explained to the owner everything about the shooting and told him I needed to check the roof. He agreed and led me up the stairway to the roof. I thanked him and got to work.

I made my way to the edge of the roof and looked across the road. Our deduction checked out; this was a perfect vantage point to shoot someone through the window of the crime scene. I could easily see Radford and the officers who were still at the window. I scoured the roof in search of anything that would be useful to crack this case. There were some faint footprints in the gravel near the edge, but they were too faint to be of any use. One thing that was odd was a small plastic pin with a silhouette of what appeared to be a witch. It was odd because it was way too early for Halloween decorations.

Then I felt a knot in my stomach. The laughing, the same pin at both crime scenes, the shootings; was this an assassination attempt against the city's councilmen and women? And the witch pins: did the party responsible for the murder attempts use them as some sort of mark of their handiwork? And then the laugh, the eerie witch laugh. Would they laugh when they believed they had killed their victims? It sounded unbelievable, but the events were too similar to just dismiss it as coincidence.

I quickly pulled out my phone and called Chief Anderson. He picked up in seconds.

"Yes Joey, what'd you find?

"Chief, I need you to call every member on the city council, board, the mayor, all 'em, and please get them to the station."

"Really? What's the matter?"

"I'll explain everything later but tell them to get to the station. I have a strong suspicion this could mean life or death."

"Alrighty, I'll do that, don't worry."

I thanked the owner for allowing me to search and quickly made my way back to Radford and the officers. This day had taken a turn for the worst.

*   *   *

5:00 PM

There was low murmuring amongst the council folk after we had explained all the events that happened. Chief Anderson stood to get the crowd's attention and spoke up.

"Ladies and gentlemen, I know you all don't want to be constantly followed by police but let me hound this fact: this could be a matter of life and death! We believe there might be an assassination attempt against each one of your lives. As a precaution, each one of you will have an officer assigned to you until we get this situation resolved."

There was a nodding of heads from the crowd showing their agreement.

"Y'all are dismissed, be careful out there, folks."

Like a group of ants, the people trailed out of the office. I followed their lead and left the office. I motioned to the rocks who were nearby to follow.

"Where are we headed?" Roc asked.

"We're going to the scene of the first assassination attempt," I replied, "I still don't know how the first attacker disappeared, so we're gonna find out for ourselves."

We made it to our car and drove to the site of the accident. It was only a few minutes' drive from the station. I parked the car on the side of the road, and we stepped out. I walked towards the last known whereabouts of the attacker, the swamp.

"We need to look around this swamp, rocks," I said, "Our suspect couldn't have vanished into thin air."

The rocks agreed, and we waded into the swamp. The swamp reached knee deep, so it wouldn't be easy to find out how the murderer vanished. We began looking amongst the reeds and tall water grasses. There was nothing of significance to be found.

"Man, this is crazy!" Roc exclaimed, "how did they just disappear?"

"I know, right?" Ks agreed, "It makes no sense..."

I knew the person couldn't have disappeared, there had to be something here. Reluctantly I began searching even deeper into the thick reeds and lily pads. As my hands pushed through the waterlogged reeds, I hit something. It felt like concrete. I pulled the reeds aside and gasped. There was a runoff drain, hidden completely out of site amongst the swamp reeds! I called to the rocks and motioned for them to come over. I took out my flashlight and motioned to the drain.

"Rocks! This must be where our first suspect disappeared," I said, "It's just large enough for a person to crawl in, so it makes sense why we couldn't find them."

"Who on earth would crawl in that dark hole?" Ks asked.

"Anyone desperate enough to get away from the police," I answered, "Let's take a look."

The rocks shrugged and walked into the drain. I got on my knees and crawled in, following them. We crawled through the slimy, dingy tube for a few minutes until we came to a large opening. This opening, I assumed, was where the drains met. The drain network was filled ankle deep with water from previous rains. The air was hot and musty. I stepped onto the sidewalk that ran along the waterway to get out of the water. Ks and Roc followed suit and got out of the water.

"Geesh, sure is wet down here!" Ks exclaimed.

I looked around the place with the flashlight and noticed a door in the grungy, concrete wall further ahead. The door led to a maintenance room. I walked down to it and looked it over. Something was off, this door should have had a lock on it, but the lock was gone. I handed Roc my derringer and nodded.

"Cover me as I open it," I told him, "Someone might be in here."

I handed the flashlight to Ks and pulled out my Glock. One hand on the door handle, and the other holding my gun, I burst through the door.

"NOPD, everyone freeze!"

I shouted the statement just as a precaution, but I didn't expect anyone to be in the room. However, I nearly shouted in shock at the sight before me. I was sure the rocks shouted or at least nearly shouted as well.

In front of us were three middle aged women, with long, curly hair down to their waists. Their faces were covered with dust from being in the drain, but still well adorned with makeup regardless. Their nails were long, and they were dressed in odd clothing, almost tunic-like dresses.

Their surroundings were odd as well. The maintenance room was equipped with a few dim lights, and a makeshift bed was in one corner of the room. I believed the women made that bed all on their own. Beside the bed were provisions: blankets, canned food, bottled water, and clothes. One of the women was on the bed, bandaged up. I knew instantly she was the person who disappeared from the car wreck. Beside the bed were two tables, one was covered in medical equipment. The other had magazines, a small radio, and to my shock, a few guns and a pile of the same witch silhouette pins!

"What is the meaning of this!?" one of the women cried.

"You two, get on the ground and spread your hands!" I exclaimed, "You on the bed, stay still and don't move!"

The injured woman raised her head looking for something but stopped immediately when she saw our guns. I took out my pair of handcuffs and handed my back up pair to Ks."

Roc, cover us as we cuff them," I said.

Roc nodded and aimed his derringer at the two on the floor. Ks and I cautiously walked up to them once close enough, pounced on the women and put the cuffs on them.

"You have no right to arrest us!" The women screamed over each other, "we've done no crime!"

"You're under arrest for trespassing in city property," I said, "You three have no business being here."

After we had secured the cuffs, I helped them up from the ground. I motioned to the guns and pins and spoke up.

"You are also under arrest for the attempted murders of councilmen Worth and Federman. Don't even try to argue with me, I saw the same witch pins at both crime scenes, the same ones in your possession. I'd say it's safe to assume you all wanted to mark your presence, show that were there. Not to mention the arsenal you all have here on the table."

The women opened their mouths in protest, but after hearing the evidence, they were dumbfounded. They knew they were busted.

"Why did you all try to assassinate the council members?" Roc asked.

"Ha! To prove a point," one woman spoke up, "those city officials can rot for all we care! They're making laws that only benefit themselves. What do they care about the poor and homeless, like us?"

"We may not have removed them all," the second lady chimed in, "but two is a good enough start for me!"

The three women erupted into eerie laughter which echoed throughout the chamber. The rocks and I looked at each other in shocked and somewhat disgusted confusion. Then I turned my attention to the women and grinned.

"Well, ladies, I hate to bring you the disappointing news, but both Mr. Federman and Mr. Worth are not dead. In fact, they are in the hospital now and expected to make a quick recovery. Now you have just confessed to everything I already suspected. You three are going to rot behind bars."

The smiles slowly faded from the women's faces as Roc and Ks led the two women out of the room. I helped the injured woman out, having her lean on my shoulder as we wandered through the waterways.

I radioed for a paddy wagon as well as an ambulance to be waiting for us out by the swamp. With some difficulty getting the injured woman through, we all made it out of the runoff drain and found ourselves back in the swamp. A few police cars and the paddy wagon were waiting for us, as well as the ambulance. Radford climbed out of one of the cars and was shocked at the sight of the women. Officers loaded the two into the paddy wagon while paramedics helped the injured woman onto a stretcher.

"You'll need a city employee to lead you down to the runoff tunnel's maintenance room," I told officers Richards and Garrison, "Unless you plan on crawling through the drain like we did."

"No no no," Richards laughed, "We'll see that we get someone to help us. Er...why the maintenance room in the runoff tunnel, exactly?"

"All the evidence is there," I explained, "The maintenance room was the hideout for these women. They had provisions, guns, radios, you name it. The reason we never found that accident suspect earlier today is simply because she crawled into the drain. She used a deodorizer spray to get rid of her scent, throwing the dogs off the trail. I'm fairly convinced these women were trying to assassinate members of the city council."

"Why would they ever want to do that?" Richards asked.

"Simply put; those women were unhappy with how the council addressed the city's issues. They openly admitted to that. So, they took it upon themselves to take them out of office, permanently."

"Well, I'll be doggone flabbergasted," Garrison said, removing his cap and running a hand through his hair, "I never thought I'd see such a weird turn of events in my life."

"Nor have I," Radford sighed, "what started out as a group of dissatisfied citizens ended up as something akin to violent rebellion."

There was no need to say anything more. All we could do was nod our heads in agreement.

-Joey Packard

# The López Sapphire

Tuesday, 1:20 PM  September 2025

The wind whistled outside the building; the lightning spread through the sky like thin, crooked fingers, which were followed by crackling, roaring thunder. The windows were white with spray of the rain. It was a typical September thunderstorm in New Orleans. Radford and I were busy sorting files at the New Orleans Police Department.

"That sure is some storm out there," Radford said, looking up from a document, "it seems like it's gonna blow through the windows!"

"Quite right," I agreed, "we've been getting a lot of nasty storms these last few weeks. Hopefully this storm dies down soon."

Our conversation was interrupted by another crack of thunder. The rain began to thin out, but the strong winds were still blowing. Radford and I resumed our work, but we were interrupted once again. This time, by Roc. Radford and I jumped as he burst into the room.

"Chief Anderson needs you two in his office," Roc exclaimed, "It sounds like a robbery case!"

Radford and I put down our work and quickly left the room. We made our way down the halls of the station and came to the chief's office. Chief Anderson was behind the desk sifting through his papers. He looked up as we entered through the door.

"Gentleman," he boomed, "we have a robbery on our hands, a rather expensive robbery. The millionaire from Spain, Mr. Antonio López, and his wife, Elena, called us about 10 minutes ago and reported that their prize jewel from Kashmir, India, has been stolen."

"Oh dear," said Radford, "That was one of the most beautiful sapphires I've ever seen."

"Indeed," agreed Chief Anderson, "a great pity. That's exactly why a thief would want to get their hands on it. Captain Sharon and her officers are already at the López mansion in District 6, and the crime scene hasn't been touched. All suspects are accounted for as well. You two better hurry on down there, good luck gentlemen."

Chief Anderson nodded a goodbye to us. Radford and I left the office and headed to our car, with the rocks following behind. The rain was still falling hard, so we dashed through the downpour to the car. I pulled my trench coat collar up and Radford held his hat on his head as we tried to shield off the rain.

"Wow, that's some storm!" Radford exclaimed as he slammed the car door shut.

I shut my door and brushed the water out of my hair, "Seems like the sky broke open," I agreed, "we're gonna get the seats all wet."

"Too late, we already did," said Roc, he and Ks were sitting in the back seats dripping wet, "we accidentally stepped in a puddle on our way in."

I pushed the button to the ignition, and it hummed to life. We pulled out of the police department parking lot and sped towards District 6, to the López mansion.

*   *   *

1:30 PM

We pulled up to López's mansion a few minutes later. The mansion was a massive, two-story structure from the 19th century. The color was a bright white, with blue trim.

Several police cars were parked outside the mansion in the round driveway. Captain Sharon of the 6th district was standing outside the mansion under the porch. Mr. and Mrs. López were talking to her, motioning quite frantically. I pulled up behind the line of police cruisers and parked the car. We ran through the still-pouring rain and bounded up the steps of the mansion. We shook our clothes under the shelter of the porch as Mr. López came hastily over to us.

"I'm so sorry to be bringing you out in this rain, Senior Weston," he said as he aided Radford, wiping his coat off, "It's just that it is very special to me and Elena here."

"No problem at all, Mr. López," Radford replied, "we're happy to be of assistance."

"The crime scene hasn't been disturbed, Radford," Captain Sharon spoke up, "And all the suspects are still here and accounted for. Well, I should say the suspect is still here."

"Oh?" I asked, "Only one person was present?"

"Yes," Mrs. López said, "Our maid, Patty, is here. She is the one who found out it was stolen." Patty was well known as the loyal maid of the López family, having served them for nearly a decade.

Officers Claire and Richards were nearby, and they led us into the mansion, as Mr. and Mrs. López continued their discussion with Captain Sharon. It was a relief to be indoors, especially after being out in the rain. From the looks of things inside the mansion, all seemed normal, other than a few officers talking to the maid, Patty. You wouldn't think a robbery had just occurred.

"Huh, doesn't look like a lot happened here," Ks said, as he looked around the building, "But duties are duties! Roc and I brought the 'crime scene' tape."

He held the roll at one end and Roc grabbed the other end; they began stringing the yellow tape all around the room, closing off certain areas of the house. Radford and I stepped over the tape and made our way towards Patty and the officers.

Patty was a short, fair lady in her mid-50's. She wore the traditional maid attire, all but for the bonnet. She was not only a reliable maid to the family, but also their good friend.

"Good evening, ma'am," I said, "Radford and I are here to hear your side of the story."

Patty stood wringing her hands very nervously and her face was white as a sheet. She was very troubled by the whole matter.

"I-I can't believe it happened," stuttered Patty, "the sapphire has been here for several months without anyone trying to steal it...I-I have been loyal to them for years...I would never..."

"Now, now," Radford said, "Let's not start that talk, we're gonna listen to your side of the story before we start making accusations. "

"Right, right," Patty took a deep breath, "well, today started off as any usual day would. After I served Mr. and Mrs. López breakfast, I hurried to finish the dishes and laundry. Mr. López's insurance agent, Mr. Daniels, was coming over to discuss an insurance plan for his recently constructed steel plant."

"At what time did this take place?" Radford asked as he wrote down the details.

"Around 11:00 p.m., he was coming to discuss the matter over lunch. So, I was pretty busy getting everything ready for his arrival. He and Mr. López talked for about an hour over the food I had prepared for them."

"When did you notice the jewel was missing?" I asked.

"Right when Mr. López asked me to fetch the jewel from their bedroom. He wanted to show Mr. Daniels the pride of his collection. The jewel, which was usually stored in a locked case, wasn't in the case! I searched the whole room top to bottom, but it wasn't anywhere to be found. I quickly ran downstairs and told the Lópezs, who were shocked. They ran to the room and began frantically searching for the sapphire, but it was hopeless. That's when they called the police."

Radford rubbed his chin, "Hmm....interesting. We are still gonna have to search you, Patty. You know the protocol."

"Please do, Detective Weston, I understand the procedures."

Officer Claire led Patty to the next room, while Radford, the rocks, and I headed upstairs to López's room. The room was relatively in order, there were no signs of a break-in. The large Victorian bed sat near the wall in the middle of the room. A large chestnut desk was left of the bed, while another small desk was to the right of the bed. The room was adorned with various red and brown drapes, curtains, and tablecloths. I took a thorough look around the room.

"Hmmm...this will be a tough one. No signs of break-in, no lead to follow."

"Indeed," Radford agreed, "But we know some thieves can be very careful to cover their tracks. Let's dust for fingerprints."

"Unless it's an inside job," I suggested.

Radford looked at me, "That would mean it was Patty who stole the sapphire."

"Maybe, but we can't rule that possibility out," I added.

Radford pulled the dusting equipment out of his coat pocket, and we got to work, dusting items that were most likely to be touched frequently. After we had a few samples, we handed them over to Officer Davis, and he headed to the station so the samples could be analyzed.

"Well, not much we can do there until we get the results back," I said as we both watched the patrol car drive off into the downpouring sheets of rain.

Radford nodded, "Yep, until then, let's continue the investigation of the room."

We headed back up to the bedroom to continue the investigation. If this was an outside job, the main thing we had to focus on was how the thief got in to begin with. Also, the drawer that held the sapphire. How did the thief break into the drawer without a key, and without leaving any sign of damage on the drawer? I looked to the window; it was still shut.

"The thief could have taken the window," I tugged on the latch, "But this latch is still locked. The only way to find out is to search for footprints outside the window."

I turned to the rocks, "Ks, Roc, go outside and search under the window for prints. Also, check for any signs of climbing up the wall. We are in a second story room, so the thief would have to climb up here."

"Right!" agreed the rocks, and dropping their tape roll, they ran downstairs and out into the rain.

"There should be mud tracks on the ground if the thief came in through the window," Radford said as he examined the ground, "but I don't see any."

I rubbed my chin, "Hmmm...you're right. Unless the thief knocked his shoes off somehow, there should be mud here. Let's use the SD to scan for footprints."

We scanned for several minutes, but there was no footprint residue coming from the window. Only a few pairs came in and out through the door, most likely the López's. At that moment, Officer Claire came in with Patty. Patty was still nervous, but she had calmed down tremendously since we first saw her.

"We searched Patty and her room," Claire said, "both searches came out clean."

An idea came to my mind, "Patty, you said Mr. Daniels was here for an hour over food. Did he ever leave the table and go near this room?"

"Well, Mr. Daniels did leave the table and head to the washroom before he ate," Patty answered, "but he was only gone for a few minutes."

"Hmmm...that does give him a window of time to come up here."

"But Mr. Packard, the only ones who have access to the drawer are the López's and me. And Mr. López handed me the keys before I went up to their bedroom, so there's no way he could have used them."

I pondered on this for a moment; could Mr. Daniels have really sneaked into the López's room and stolen the sapphire, all in the span of a few minutes? It wasn't impossible, but he would have to be very quick and stealthy, as well as a skilled locksmith. To be able to get through the locks without damaging the drawer proved that. Any immature thief would have left some sign of tampering on the locks.

Patty was allowed to return to the lobby. Radford and I followed as we headed back through the hall. As we walked through the hall, I tried to gather as much information as I could. There wasn't anything noteworthy, besides a few tables in the hall, containing items such as vases and books. A shelf next to the kitchen doorway contained a classic wash basin, a retro can opener, and a jar labeled "gluten free flour." I heard Radford ask Patty why there was flour in the hall instead of the kitchen. She simply said they just don't use it in a while since it's gluten free. It was the flour that she used to cook for the guests who were allergic to gluten, so it was stored in the hall to save space in the kitchen.

As we made it to the lobby, the rocks came in, dripping wet.

"No luck there," Roc explained, "The ground is all mud, if there were any footprints, the rain washed it all way."

"Spigots," I muttered, "That doesn't help us."

"All we can do now is wait until we get the results from the fingerprint dustings," Radford added, " We'll have to wait a couple days for that process to be complete."

We agreed no more could be done until we got the results back. The López's were disappointed by it all, but they understood the police protocol. The rain had finally let up as we left the mansion. We walked back to the car, as the sun's golden rays pierced through the clouds, chasing away the gloom.

*　*　*

Wednesday, 11: 10 AM

Radford and I were in the office trying to figure out all the evidence we gathered the previous day. The results from the fingerprints had not come back yet. The only thing we could do was try to figure out how the sapphire was stolen from the evidence we had.

"Still not much to go by," Radford grumbled, "Not enough evidence to make an accurate deduction."

I nodded, "We can't do anymore with what we have. Exactly why I plan to have a visit with Mr. Daniels soon."

Radford looked up, "You think he stole the sapphire?"

"It's a hunch right now, but he's our only other suspect."

"Hmmm...that is true. You plan on meeting him today?"

I checked my watch, "Right now actually. Best to ask the questions before the case gets cold."

Radford nodded and went back to sorting the evidence. I grabbed my coat, leaving the evidence room. I passed our office and called to the rocks; they were busy sorting paperwork.

"Come along, you two. We got an appointment with a one certain Mr. Daniels."

Ks and Roc looked at each other and shrugged. They dropped their files and followed me out of the department.

"Uh, shouldn't we be working on the case?" Roc asked.

"We are," I replied, "We're going to get Mr. Daniels side of the story."

*   *   *

11:20 AM

We pulled up to Mr. Daniels' office ten minutes later. We were just on time as we saw Mr. Daniels leave his work, heading out for lunch. We clambered out of the car and hurried after him down the sidewalk.

"Mr. Daniels," I called out, "We would like to speak with you."

Mr. Daniels stopped walking and turned to us, "Detective Packard, this is a pleasant surprise."

115

"Mr. Daniels, we have a few questions to ask you about the sapphire stolen from the Lópezs."

"Ah, the sapphire," Mr. Daniels sighed, "That's a shame, it truly was a beautiful piece of jewelry."

"Do you mind if we tag along with you for lunch?"

"Of course not, I was just headed to Brennan's right now."

With a turn of his heel, Mr. Daniels resumed his stride to the restaurant and the rocks and I followed him. After a few minutes' walk, we made it to Brennan's. The rocks waited outside while Mr. Daniels and I found ourselves a seat inside. The waiter set down two glasses of water and an appetizer of breadsticks. He gave us a few minutes to look at our menus.

"Breadstick?" I asked, sliding the basket over to him.

"Oh, no thank you, Mr. Packard," he chuckled, "I only eat gluten-free foods, which is why I come here for lunch often. The folks here are kind enough to make my food gluten-free."

"Ah, forgive my ignorance," I said, making sure to get back to the discussion of the sapphire, "Right. You had lunch with Mr. López last night right before the sapphire was stolen?"

"Correct," he replied, "though, we didn't get around to lunch before the incident struck."

"I see. You were also getting down to business about insurance coverage on a new steel plant, I assume?"

"Right. The insurance matters were dropped immediately as well. Mr. López was too distraught after the theft of his prized sapphire to discuss further business matters. Who wouldn't be?"

"Hmmm...of course. You didn't happen to go up to the López's bedroom at any time yourself, did you?"

"No, sir, I did not. In fact, I never laid eyes on sapphire. The only time I did get up was to wash up in the wash..."

I cut him off immediately and sat up straight in my chair. That's it! The thief was in our midst the whole time while we were investigating the crime scene! And we almost let them get away, right under our very noses. I quickly got out of my chair and put on my coat. Mr. Daniels was surprised.

"Hey, Packard, where are you going? We didn't even get our meals!"

"Sorry for leaving so soon, Mr. Daniels," I said, heading out the door, "but I may have found who the thief is and how they stole the sapphire."

"Oh, well, good luck!" he called out.

I swiftly stepped through the door, passing the rocks. The rocks followed me to the car.


Ks scratched his head, "That was a quick lunch..."

"Rocks, I may just have had a breakthrough," I replied and gave Roc my phone, "Roc, call Captain Sharon and the boys. Tell them to meet us at the López's mansion."

Roc looked puzzled, but he did as I said. We clambered back into the car and drove as fast as the law allowed us to the mansion. I was feeling quite optimistic; I was sure I had solved the case.


*   *   *


11:35 AM

It took just a few minutes to drive from Brennan's to López's mansion. We pulled in and I parked the car. The rocks hopped out and quickly followed me up the steps.

"Why the rush?" Roc asked, "The house will still be here whether we walk or run."

"The house will be, but the sapphire might not..." I replied.

I pounded the lever on the door and waited. After a few moments, the sound of latches could be heard behind the door. Patty's face peeked through the crack. She instantly opened the door when she recognized it was us.

"Mr. Packard," she said looking a little startled, "I didn't expect you to be back so early? Did you get the fingerprints results?"

"Not exactly," I grinned, "but I believe I found the culprit. I've already called Mr. and Mrs. López. They'll be over here shortly."

"O-oh, sure, good. Come in, please." She opened the door and let us in.

Patty went back to the kitchen, and I quickly explained my theory and plan to the rocks. It had only been a few minutes when the Lópezs and the police arrived. I had the rocks go up to both the López's and Patty's room while we were waiting. They knew what they had to do and ran up to the rooms while Patty was cleaning the kitchen. Captain Sharon, Radford, and Officers Herman and Paul followed the Lópezs up the steps. The Lópezs looked very enthusiastic while anxious at the same time. I opened the door for them since Patty was in the kitchen.

"Did you find it?" Mr. López asked while giving me a firm but quick handshake, "Did you find the sapphire?"

"That will all be answered in due time," I reassured him. I turned to all of them, "Now, everyone, come with me to the living room, I will explain how it all happened."

We all arrived at the living room. The Lópezs and Radford took a seat around the coffee table while Officers Pual and Herman stood near the window. Captain Sharon had fetched Patty from the kitchen to join us. I stepped in front of them and took a deep breath.

"Ladies and gentlemen, I believe I have deduced who the criminal is. The thief was among us the entire time. They had quite the nerve to pull off this act."

There was a long pause of silence in the room, followed by whispers amongst the group. They turned their attention back to me so I could finish. I looked to the back of the room.

"Patty, would you kindly return the sapphire back to the Lópezs."

A loud gasp could be heard around the room. Patty turned white as a ghost.

"M-Mr. Packard...," she stuttered, "How could...how could you accuse me!?"

Everyone broke into chatter. The Lópezs were visibly and truly upset. Radford turned to me.

"Joey, can you prove this claim?"

"I most certainly can," I replied. I shouted to the entrance of the living room, "Rocks, you can come in now!"

Ks and Roc walked into the living room; Roc was holding something in his hand. They both looked ecstatic.

"Well, rocks," I asked, "Have you found the sapphire?"

Roc nodded and grinned, "Yep, we have it right here. We found it stuffed into a pair of rolled up stockings in Patty's drawer."

The group turned their attention to the rocks. Roc unraveled the pair of stockings and pulled out a shimmering, blue object: the sapphire. Everyone was shocked, including myself to a small degree. There still was that nagging bit of doubt in the back of my head about whether Patty had it or not.

"The sapphire! You found the sapphire!" Mr. López exclaimed and got up from his seat. He rushed to the rocks and Roc handed him the sapphire. Mr. López beamed, "This is definitely our sapphire!"

His beam quickly turned into the most disappointing frown. Mrs. López stood up as well and turned to Patty.

"Patty, why did you steal it?" she asked, "why did you steal the sapphire? "

"And after we treated you so well for years," Mr. López added, "we were friends for a long time."

Patty tried to speak, but the words didn't come out. Radford turned to me, "How did you find out she took it?"

"It was actually Mr. Daniels who unknowingly helped me solve it," I answered, "while we were at lunch, he said he only ate gluten-free foods. Patty either stumbled last night or she lied when she told us that the gluten-free flour jar was not used in a while. That would be incorrect if Mr. Daniels just ate with them, so I knew that the jar was used recently."

"My word," said Radford, "but still, how did she even steal the sapphire?"

"That's where the jar comes in once again," I continued, "when Mr. López told

Patty to get the sapphire for him, she decided to act. And there is no better way to hide the sapphire than sticking it in the flour jar left in the hallway up to the bedrooms. Unfortunately for her, her plan was interrupted when she heard footsteps coming towards her. It happened to be only Mr. Daniels heading to the washroom. Out of panic, she decided to fabricate the story of the sapphire being stolen. An amateur mistake, she would have been better off if she remained quiet. The reason the lock was never tampered with was because she unlocked it with the key. And it almost worked. Patty nearly fooled all of us."

The Lópezs were at a loss for words. Mr. López looked at Patty. "Patty, I'm...I'm speechless!"

"I...I didn't do any of that!" Patty finally spoke up, "I...I don't know how it disappeared and reappeared in my drawer, but I didn't take the jewel! I'm honest!"

"What about the flour?" Mr. López asked.

"I'm honest, sir, I left it in the hall to save space in the kitchen...I didn't stash the jewel away in the jar!"

"The jewel was in your possession, Patty," Captain Sharon said, "I'm sorry, Patty, but we have no choice but to charge you with taking it."

"Patty..." Mrs. López began, but she remained silent and looked down to the floor.

Officer Pual walked behind Patty and put the handcuffs on her. "Come along now," he said as he clicked the cuffs in place, "Let's go."

He, Herman, and Captain Sharon lead Patty out of the mansion. The Lópezs followed them. They would now have to do the tedious work of signing papers and going to court. Radford was still rather surprised by the turnout. I didn't blame him, I was quite disappointed as well, even though my theory had turned out to be true.

"I can't believe she would steal it," Radford said as he put his hat on his head, "she seemed like a charming, kind, and innocent woman. Someone who the Lópezs trusted for a long time."

I pat Radford on the back as we and the rocks walked out of the mansion. "Well, sometimes even the most innocuous people are the most devious. They use their charm and innocence as a shield."

"Heh, I guess I shouldn't be all that amazed about that," Radford chuckled, "I've been in this field of work for 30 years, and yet I'm still surprised by some of the things I see."

I nodded; I couldn't agree more.

-Joey Packard

# The Opium Trade

The sun's warm rays streamed through the large office windows, bouncing off the leather chairs and wooden furniture. It was quickly getting chilly this time of year, nearly January. The sun felt good while the air outside the NOPD station was becoming quite cold.

"Mmmm!" Radford smacked his lips, "Nothing like leftover Christmas pumpkin pie in the morning."

"Mhmm," I agreed taking another bite, "Mrs. Woods sure knows how to bake some wonderful pie."

"That was quite a Christmas banquet, I must say," Radford set his fork down and washed the pie down with a cup of apple cider, "It was quite a full park, and even our friend from the auto shop showed up, Scooter."

"Yep," I replied, "And so did those two young chaps, Ricky and Tommy Lee."

"Yes, and it was nice of the López family to buy those turkeys and hams for the banquet. We still have leftovers days later..."

Officer Richards tapped on the door post of our office and interrupted us," Radford, Joey, sorry to interrupt your pleasant morning, but Anderson needs you two."

"It was a pleasant morning," Radford grumbled as he stood up, "Until circumstances said otherwise."

Chief Anderson was a little on edge when we entered his office. He seemed to be more jovial than usual, which was surprising to us. He looked up quickly as we entered and slammed a stack of papers on his desk.

"Gentleman," he boomed with a grin, "we believe we just uncovered a major smuggling ring trying to extend its operations into New Orleans!"

"How did you come across that?" Radford asked.

"The boys at the Harbor Police Department have been noticing unusual activity around the harbor," Anderson replied, "The harbor master received a message from a ship a few miles offshore, wanting to come inland. The ship specified the weight and product they were carrying. The harbor master called us about this, since he was a little skeptical. He wasn't expecting any shipments today. So, we sent out some of the harbor police to check it out. They came back with a report, and in that report, they were given a different weight than what the ship's captain told the harbor master. Either it was a slip-up, or there's something on that ship they don't want us knowing about. It could be narcotics, guns, who knows."

"So, you are gonna have us go to the harbor and arrest them on arrival," I asked.

"Not yet" Anderson replied, "we have no real concrete evidence yet, only assumptions, which is exactly why I'm sending both of you to the harbor. I've already alerted the Harbor police of your arrival. Chief Allen of the Harbor Police should be expecting you. Good luck."

"Thanks, Chief," Radford said, and we both left the office. We passed the rocks on our way out.

"Rocks!" I called, "You two are coming with us."

"Oh," they asked, "where we goin'?"

"To the harbor, we're meeting up with the Harbor police department."

The rocks raised their hands as if to protest, but they both sighed and followed anyway.

*　　*　　*

11:12 AM

The air had become rather cold now, it was winter after all. New Orleans has never had snow since the late 1800s, but we do get cold winters. Radford and I pulled on our coats before we stepped out of our warm car into the brisk, chilly air. As soon as I opened the door, the bone-chilling wind flew through the car, instantly sucking out all the warm air. Radford shivered and pulled up his coat cuff.

"Brrrr! It's getting colder every day," he chattered.

We left the vehicle and made our way across the harbor to the Harbor Police

Department. The smell of the salty air penetrated our nostrils, and the seagulls hollered overhead. Inside the Harbor Police Department, Chief Allen was waiting for us. He was a dark-skinned man with a tall build, and a black goatee settled itself right in the middle of his chin.

"Gentleman," he looked up from his desk, "Glad you could make it."

"Not a problem at all Allen," Radford said as we both shook Allen's hand, "Do you have any plans of action?"

"I do indeed," Allen continued, "We need you and Joey to get an inside look at that cargo ship. We need to be certain that they are carrying illegal goods before we make any arrests."

Chief Allen turned to a young officer who was in the room with us. "Landon, could you please get the dossier from the file room."

"Yes chief," said the young officer, and he left into the next room. Radford and I watched as he left.

"That's one of my new recruits," said the chief, regaining our attention, "he applied a few days ago, but I digress. Our detectives from the investigation division are at the scene already. I wish you gentlemen good luck."

The rookie came back with the flies and handed them to Radford and me. We took the files and headed out the door.

It was only a six-minute drive from the harbor department to the Port of New Orleans. At a distance away from us, Detective Sean and Detective Owen were standing outside the ship on the docks, disguised as ordinary dock workers. Next to them was the harbor master of the Port. A boat ramp was laid down from the boat to the docks. Large, yellow cranes on track wheels were rolling into place, ready to unload the cargo from the ship.

"It seems we are going undercover," Radford said, adjusting his coat, "make sure your police badge is completely hidden. The sailors shouldn't recognize us...unless they see the rocks."

"Right, I nodded, "That's why they aren't gonna be with us. Instead..."

I turned to the rocks, "Ks, Roc, you two are going to scope out the cargo in the hold."

I gave Roc my phone and Ks a miniature flashlight, "Take pictures of any contraband you find. Make sure no one sees you or the whole thing is a bust."

The rocks nodded and ran away, attempting to find a secluded entry point to the ship. I turned my attention back to Radford and the two detectives. They were discussing plans on their next actions after we boarded.

"Okay," Sean began, "Owen and I will go to down to the cargo hold as 'workers.' You two will act out as harbor master's associates."

"That's the plan Chief Allen had in mind," Owen added, "we will all meet at that blue warehouse at 12:00."

"Alright gentlemen," the harbor master spoke up, "It's time we'd better be joining the captain."

Radford and I nodded, and we all made our way up the gang plank. The harbor master led the way up the plank. The captain of the ship was waiting and extended his hand.

"Welcome aboard gentlemen," he said with a sly smile, "coming to inspect the cargo I assume?"

"we are sir," the harbor master replied, shaking his hand, "I have a few of my associates here to carry out the inspection."

"Good, good," the captain said, "I assure you everything is in order and anything that doesn't belong is not on board."

"That's good for us," the harbor master clasped his hands together, "Makes our job all the easier!"

The captain then led us to his cabin while Owen and Sean went down to the hold to play their part as inspectors. We then went through all the ship's logs, records of its destinations, and the cargo it held. One thing was to be noted, the weight recorded was still lower than the actual weight of the cargo recorded by the harbor police. We knew there was something on this ship that shouldn't belong there. After about an hour in the captain's cabin, we left the ship and made our way back onto the dock. We walked to our meeting spot and waited for Owen and Sean. After a few minutes, both detectives walked out of the ship and joined us.

"Well," asked the harbor master, "did you find anything?"

Sean took off his plainclothes cap, "Nothing that we could verify. All the cargo is legal steel goods. We didn't find anything illegal."

"You would never find it that way even if you tried!" called Roc as he and Ks both ran to us.

"What do you two know about this?" Owen asked, "What'd you find?"

"The illegal cargo was never in the hold," Ks explained, "well, the main hold that is. Roc and I saw a few men head down to the hold frantically while you all were coming aboard. They seemed to be very panicked and worried about something. So, we followed them down to the hold. Except, they only went deeper, down beyond the hold."

"You mean a secret, second hold?" Radford asked.

"Right you are," Ks continued, "Below was a smaller hold with at least a dozen or more crates in them. Roc and I waited until the coast was clear before we checked out the crates. And when they left, we made our move. We discovered that this ship is carrying opium."

There was a little gasp among the group. "Opium? Are you sure it was opium?" I asked.

"You can see for yourself," said Roc as he handed me my phone, "It's it a good thing we had this to take pictures."

I flipped through the pictures on the phone. The rocks were right, it was opium, the blackish substance was all too familiar.

"That explains the difference in the weights," the harbor master spoke up.

"Another thing," said Roc, "we overheard where they are gonna store it."

He pointed to a small blue shed further down the docks. It seemed to be out of commission due to its dilapidated condition.

"They have arranged for the crates to be stored there in the shed while the main cargo is being stored in the warehouse," Roc continued, "that way they wouldn't be noticed, or at least suspected, by the harbor master. They are gonna carry it to the shed from the ship in a small, white delivery truck. "

"And," Ks added, "the captain and the opium smugglers are gonna meet up in the warehouse's office building. The smugglers are members of a group from different parts of the world, some from India, China, Africa, even Europe."

"Sounds like a world organization," I said.

"We'd better report this to Chief Allen immediately," Radford said, "If we hurry, we'll still have time to catch them."

*   *   *

12:25 PM

Chief Allen was enthusiastic about the news. We had uncovered ourselves a drug ring, and his department had discovered it! We offered our congratulations to him as we arrived at his department.

Thank you, gentlemen," Allen held up his hands, "but we still have to catch them, let's not celebrate quite yet!"

"You're right," I agreed, "They're not behind bars yet. What's the next step, Allen?"

"Stakeouts," replied Allen, "We know they are gonna be dropping the opium off at that abandoned shed, and we also know they will be meeting in the harbor warehouse office. Tonight, my boys are gonna confiscate the cargo in the delivery truck at the shed after it's been unloaded. Joey, you and Radford will be waiting for them in the office building. We'll radio you two when we secure the drug truck."

"Sounds like a plan," Radford said, "we'll nab these smugglers yet!"

*   *   *

7:45 PM

*Creeeek!* I slowly opened the office door and peered in. It was all dark and empty;

the drug gang wasn't here yet. I slowly stepped through the door and motioned for Radford and the rocks to follow.

"We came at a good time," I whispered, "they aren't here yet."

"Splendid!" Radford exclaimed.

We sure got the edge," I said as I pulled out my gun, "but still, we should be really cautious."

"Right," Radford pulled out his revolver and muttered, "Let's hope we don't have to use these."

"We can sit in the corner near the desk," I pointed to a dark corner, hidden from the streetlights, "it's out of view from the door and we can get the jump on them easier."

We hunkered down in the corner and waited. I checked the time; it was 7:50. The group would be here in ten minutes, and we would be there to grab them. The time slowly dragged along through the night. Fifteen minutes passed, then thirty. Radford shivered and pulled up his coat cuff.

"Brrr! It's getting beastly cold, what's taking them so long?"

"Beats me," I replied, "they might have been delayed."

Just then, Chief Allen's voice came over the walkie talkie in Radford's coat.

"Radford, Joey, this is Allen. We caught them! My men were watching as a few workers loaded the crates into their getaway truck. We managed to nab the truck before it could leave the port. Have you managed to capture the lead smugglers yet?"

"Not yet, Allen," Radford responded, "They must be delayed or something."

"Hold your post, they are bound to turn up soon."

Radford put the talkie back in his coat. I cupped my hands and blew warm air into them.

"Let's hope they do show up," I said, rubbing my hands together vigorously, "It's getting dang cold pretty quick."

Radford pulled out two pairs of gloves and handed me a pair, "I hope so too, I hate sitting out here freezing."

Another fifteen minutes passed by, and another; an hour had gone by since we first arrived. Radford was spinning the barrel to his revolver, hoping that would pass the time just a bit quicker. I pulled out my gun and stood up.

"Well, it seems they aren't coming in here," I said, "Let's take a look around this building."

Radford slapped the barrel back into his gun and stood up, "Right, let's go."

I pointed to the room down a hall, "There's a room down that hall, let's check it out."

We slowly and methodically made our way down the hall to the room. I cautiously opened the door and stuck my hand in, feeling along the wall for a light switch. I felt one and switched it on. The bright light pierced the darkness like a beam of sunlight. Radford and I blinked for a bit, adjusting our eyes to the light. After we could see clearly, we looked around the room. Empty.

"I don't get it," Radford scratched his head, "They were supposed to be here at eight, why aren't they here?"

"Beats me," I replied. I turned to the rocks, "Unless our friends here heard wrong..."

"Woah, woah, woah!" Ks said defensively, "What's this, throwing accusations?"

"Trust us," Roc said, "we heard them clearly as we hear you now. Besides, the delivery van came on time as we heard too, but not the agents for some reason..."

I thought about that for a moment, "Hmmm...It seems like a last-minute ditch-out..."

"Well, we can't stand here waiting for people who aren't coming," said Radford, "we best better head back to the station and report this to Allen. I have a feeling the poor chap's gonna be disappointed..."

* * *

9:13 PM

Saying Chief Allen was going to be disappointed was an understatement. The guy lost all the charisma and good-natured

149

spirit he possessed only a few hours earlier. Radford attempted to cheer him up.

"Hey Allen, now it's not all bad. We managed to stop the opium shipment before it got distributed throughout all of New Orleans."

"That still ain't that much of a win for us..." Allen sighed with a wave of his hand, "when the perpetrators who are running this organization are running around New Orleans scot-free."

"I just want to know how they found out we were coming," I chimed in, "Obviously they knew the law was there waiting for them and they booked it."

"But if they knew we were there, why did they still try to deliver the opium?" Roc asked.

"Maybe they couldn't get the message to the truck drivers in time," I suggested,

"The organization leaders probably barely had any time to get out themselves."

Chief Allen slumped back into his chair, "You're free to go gentlemen, tell Anderson thanks for sending you both over."

Radford and I nodded as we and the rocks left the chief alone to his disappointment. Walking down the hall of the department, we discussed and questioned the puzzling events that just happened.

"How on the green earth did those scumbags know we were there?" asked Ks.

"That's what I'd like to know," I rubbed my chin, "It's almost like there was a mole in our own departments, but that can't be possible. All of our people are honest, good working people."

"Are they?" Radford asked.

That simple question caused a moment of silence. I finally broke the silence, "What do you have in mind?"

"I'd like to take a look at the security footage from Chief Allen's office," Radford simply stated.

I looked at the rocks, they looked at me. We three were shocked! Was Radford really implying that Chief Allen was behind the opium trade? I doubted that's what he really meant; it was way too big of an accusation. Radford walked to the reception desk. The man behind the desk gazed up at us.

"Ah, Mr. Weston, Mr. Packard. You both leaving us?"

"Not quite yet, my good man," Radford replied, "I'd like to have a look at the security footage from Chief Allen's office and the rooms in close proximity to it."

I could see by the look of the desk receptionist's face that he too was confused.

"Sure, right away, Mr. Weston," he finally blurted out, "follow me."

We followed him back down the hall to the security room. I was genuinely baffled at what Radford was trying to get at. I was also surprised by how serious his mood was. When we arrived at the security room, the desk receptionist opened the door to the room and allowed us in. We entered the room, and he closed the door behind us.

"Alrighty," Radford said, clasping his hands together. He turned to me, "Joey, pull up the footage from the moment we discussed our plans with Chief Allen."

I nodded and began scrolling through the footage. After a bit of searching, I came upon the moment when we first met Allen in the morning. We both got comfy in our chairs and observed the footage. The rocks clambered up on the desk to get a better look. We watched the whole footage through until the moment that Radford and I left.

"Did anything particular stand out in that meeting?" Radford asked.

"Not really," I answered, "Except, maybe for the part where the chief told the officer to get him the dossier from the file room."

"Exactly," Radford beamed, "Now, play the footage from the file room. Make sure it's around the same time, around 11:15a.m."

"How will that explain anything?" Ks asked.

"You'll see," Radford grinned, "We have our culprit."

I pulled up the footage from the exact moment Chief Allen told the rookie cop to get the dossier. The rookie did go to the file room as told, but he didn't get the file the chief wanted. Instead, he hid behind the wall at the entrance of the adjacent room and stood still.

"Wait," Roc observed, "he seems to be listening in on our conversation!"

"Exactly what I expected," Radford rose from his seat and pointed to the screen, "Look, he's also recording our discussion with his phone!"

"So, he wasn't just a new officer," I said, "He was a spy for the opium smugglers! They knew we would pick them up eventually, so they sent him in here to record our every move."

"Well, if he recorded the message, why did the delivery truck still come to the planned pick-up spot?" Ks asked.

"Perhaps," I replied, "he didn't have enough time to warn them. Maybe he only had enough time to either warn the delivery truck or the leaders of the organization. Obviously, the leaders being more important, he chose them and was able to warn them."

"We must tell Chief Allen at once," Radford said heading for the door, "and we'd better throw that new officer behind some steel bars!"

*  *  *

Tuesday, 11:30 AM

We nabbed the rookie early, around seven in the morning, as he came into work. We took his phone and tried to find the recording, but he obviously deleted it. He also didn't confess to ever recording us, so we held him in a cell until we could get the data from his phone. Chief Allen was even

**156**

more disappointed that one of his new recruits was working for the smugglers, but he was also optimistic that the phone would have some new evidence in it. We had the phone sent to the department's digital forensic analyst, hoping the specialist would be able to retrieve the data. It has been a few hours since we sent the device over, and we were expecting a visit from the specialist any minute now. At that moment, an officer knocked on Chief Allen's door post.

"The specialist is here, sir," the officer said, "he managed to retrieve the recording and even more evidence against the rookie."

Allen, Radford, and I all sat up in our chairs. "Show him in!" Allen beamed.

The officer waved the specialist in. He greeted us and set the phone on the chief's desk.

"He's right," he began, "we found the recording as well as a good amount of other evidence on the leaders of this organization."

The chief perked up instantly, "By George! We have a chance!"

"So, you mean all hope isn't lost?" Ks asked, "We can still find those smugglers?"

"We just might," Radford replied, "we have their faces and names, but New Orleans is a big city. They could be here in this city, or they could be in any other city. Only time will tell..."

I could only agree.

-Joey Packard